CATHERINE
CERTITUDE

CATHERINE CERTITUDE

PATRICK MODIANO

Illustrated by

Jean-Jacques Sempé

Translation by William Rodarmor

Andersen Press · London

This edition first published in 2020 by
Andersen Press Limited
20 Vauxhall Bridge Road
London SW1V 2SA
www.andersenpress.co.uk

2 4 6 8 10 9 7 5 3 1

First published in 1988 in France
by Éditions Gallimard
First English translation published in 2001 in the United States of America
by David R. Godine, Publisher, Inc
First published in 2015 in the UK in hardback by Andersen Press Limited.

British Library Cataloguing in Publication Data available.

ISBN 978 1 78344 982 8

Printed and bound in China.

It's snowing here in New York, and I'm looking out of the window of my 59th Street apartment at the building across the way where I run a dance school. Behind the large glass panes, the students in leotards have stopped their pointe work and entrechats practice. As a change of pace, my daughter, who works as my assistant, is showing them a jazz step.

I'll join them in a few minutes.

Among the students is a little girl who wears glasses. She set them down on a chair before the lesson started, the way I used to when I was her age and taking lessons with Madame Dismailova. You don't wear glasses when you dance. I remember that when I was with Madame Dismailova, I would practise not wearing my glasses during the day. The shapes of people and things lost their sharpness and everything was blurry. Even sounds became muffled. Without my glasses, the world lost its roughness and became as soft and downy as the big pillow I used to lean my cheek against before going to sleep.

"What are you daydreaming about, Catherine?" my father would ask me. "You should put your glasses on."

I did as he said, and everything changed back to its everyday sharpness and precision. When I wore my glasses I saw the world as it was. I couldn't dream any more.

Here in New York, I belonged to a ballet company for a

few years, then taught dance lessons with my mother. When she retired, I continued without her. And now I work with my daughter. My father should retire, too, but can't bring himself to. Actually, what would he be retiring from? I never knew exactly what kind of work Papa did. He and Mama live in a small Greenwich Village apartment. We're nobody special; just New Yorkers, like so many others. Only one thing in my life is out of the ordinary: before we came to America, I spent my childhood in Paris, in a neighbourhood off the 10th *arrondissement*. That was almost thirty years ago.

We lived above a kind of shop on Hauteville Street, with a steel shutter that Papa rolled down every evening at seven.

The place looked like the luggage room of a country railway station. There were always crates and packages piled on top of one another. There was a scale, too, with an enormous platform at floor level that must have been designed for heavy loads, because the dial went up to six hundred pounds.

I never saw anything on the scale's platform. Except for Papa. At those rare moments when his partner, Mister

Casterade, was out, Papa would stand silent and still in the centre of the platform, with his hands in his pockets and his head bowed. He would thoughtfully gaze at the dial; I remember it read one hundred and seventy pounds.

Sometimes Papa would say, "Come here, Catherine," and I would join him on the scale. We would stand there, the two of us, Papa's hand on my shoulders, without moving. We looked as if we were posing for a photograph. I took off my glasses, and Papa took off his. Everything around us became soft and fuzzy. Time stopped. We felt fine.

One day Mister Casterade caught us standing on the scale.

"What are you doing?" he asked.

The spell was broken. Papa and I put our glasses back on.

"We're weighing ourselves, can't you see?" Papa said.

Without bothering to reply, Casterade trotted briskly to the office at the back of the shop. Behind a glass partition, two big walnut desks with swivel chairs faced each other: Papa's and Mister Casterade's.

Mister Casterade started working with Papa after Mama left. She's American. When she was twenty, Mama belonged to a dance troupe that came to Paris on tour. She met my father, they got married, and Mama stayed on in Paris, dancing in music halls: the Empire, the Tabarin, the Alhambra . . . I saved all the programmes. But she was homesick. After a few years, she decided to go back to America. Papa promised her we would join her there, as soon as he wrapped up his "business affairs." Or at least that was the explanation he gave me. Later on, I understood that there were other reasons for Mama's departure.

Every week, Papa and I would each get a letter from America, in envelopes bordered with little red and blue stripes.

Mama's letter always ended with: *"Catherine, all my hugs and kisses. I'm always thinking of you. Mama."*

Sometimes Mama made spelling mistakes.

When Papa talked to me about his partner Raymond Casterade, he always called him "The Pill."

"Catherine, honey, I can't pick you up at school this afternoon. I have to work all evening with 'The Pill.' "

Mister Casterade had brown hair, dark eyes, and a very long chest. In fact, his chest was so long and stiff, you couldn't see his legs moving, so he seemed to be gliding along on roller skates, or even ice skates.

Later, I learned that Papa had originally hired Mister Casterade as his secretary. He wanted someone who was good at spelling, and when he was young, Mister Casterade had got a degree in literature. Later, "The Pill" became his partner.

Mister Casterade would lecture people at the drop of a hat.

He also liked to announce catastrophes. In the morning, he would sit down at his desk and slowly open the newspaper. Papa would be sitting across from at him his desk, with his glasses off. Mister Casterade would report on the day's crimes and disasters.

"Georges, you aren't listening," Mister Casterade would scold. "You're woolgathering. You're afraid to see the world as it is. You should put your glasses on."

"Must I?" asked Papa.

"The Pill" had another odd habit, that of dictating letters.

He would do this in a loud voice with his chest puffed out. How many times did I see Papa typing business letters while Mister Casterade dictated, without daring to tell him — out of politeness — that the letters served no purpose? Mister Casterade would spell some words out and even supply punctuation marks.

As soon as his partner turned his back, Papa would rip up the letters.

"The Pill" even enjoyed dictating my homework to me, and I had to let him. Sometimes I got good marks, but usually the teacher would write "Off the subject" on my paper.

So Papa told me, "If you feel he's 'off the subject,' tear up the homework he dictated and start again on your own."

When Mister Casterade was away, Papa would imitate him:

"Semicolon, open quote, comma, colon, open parenthesis, new line, close parenthesis, close quote."

He would say all this while imitating Mister Casterade's voice, and I would dissolve into hysterics.

"Let's be serious, young lady, if you don't mind," Papa said, "Don't forget to capitalise the U. And put on your glasses, so you can see the world as it is."

One afternoon, when I was at the shop on my way home with Papa, Mister Casterade asked me to show him my report. He read it, chewing on his cigarette holder, then turned his dark eyes on me.

"Young lady," he said, "I am very disappointed. I expected better from you, especially in spelling. All that I see, reading this report, is . . ."

But I had taken off my glasses, and couldn't hear him any more.

"Be quiet, Casterade," Papa said. "You're getting on my nerves. Leave the girl alone."

"Very well."

Mister Casterade stood up, wreathed in scorn, and glided over to the office door. Then he disappeared, very erect, looking quite dignified on his invisible roller skates.

Papa and I looked at each other over the tops of our glasses.

Later on, when we were in America, the shop on Hauteville Street and Mister Casterade seemed so far away that we wondered if they had really existed. One afternoon, while we were walking in Central Park, I asked Papa why he had let Mister Casterade play such a large part in his business and our family life, to the point of letting him dictate his letters, and listening to his lectures without daring to interrupt.

"I didn't have any choice," Papa admitted. "Casterade once got me out of a real jam."

He never said any more about it. But one day, when Mister Casterade was very angry, I had heard him tell Papa:

"Georges, you should remember that your real friends are the ones who save you from the clutches of the law."

When Papa first met him, Casterade had just left his job teaching French in a suburban high school. It helped that Papa admired people who wrote books: Mister Casterade had once published several volumes of verse. I have one of his books, in the library here in my New York apartment; Papa must have stuffed it in his suitcase when we were leaving France, as a keepsake. The book is called *Cantelina* and was published by the author himself, 15 Aqueduc Street, 10th Arrondissement, Paris. A biographical note on the back cover reads, "Raymond Casterade. Laureate of the Languedoc Poetry Festival, the Mussetists of Bordeaux, and the Gascogne-North Africa Literary Association."

Above the shop front, whose large frosted-glass window kept nosy passersby on Hauteville Street from peering in, hung a sign with navy blue letters. It read: "CASTERADE & CERTITUDE Exp.–Trans." Certitude is Papa's and my last name. Here in America it's pronounced "Sir-tih-toode," which sounds odd, but it had a good French ring to it back in Paris. Papa explained to me, later, that our real name was much more complicated. Something like Tscertitscevadze, or Chercetitudjvili.

There had been just one clerk in the deserted, sunny Civil Registry office. He was about to write my father's very complicated name in the registry book when he sighed. Unconsciously, the clerk waved away a swarm of invisible bees, or mosquitoes, or crickets, as if the Cher, the Ttch, the Etit, and the Vili of my father's name felt like hundreds of insects buzzing around him.

"Your name could give a person hives," he told Papa, wiping his brow. "What if we simplified it? How about . . . 'Certitude'?"

"Whatever you say," said Papa.

"All right: Certitude."

So the shop in Hauteville Street bore the sign: "CASTERADE & CERTITUDE Exp.–Trans."

And what did "Exp.–Trans." mean? My father has always

been discreetly evasive on the subject.

Expeditions? Export? Transit? Transportation?

The work was often done at night. More than once I was awakened by the comings and goings of lorries that would pull up, leaving their motors running. From my bedroom window, I saw men carrying crates in and out of the shop. Standing on the pavement, Papa and Mister Casterade would direct this nocturnal activity. Papa held an open account book and took notes as the crates were unloaded from one lorry or loaded onto another. Among some old papers, I once found a page from that account book:

Heures	Sortie	Heures	Arrivée
10h30	Matériel radio et boulons	10h15	chaussures militaires
11h.	chemises, vis et chandails	11h15	imperméables
11h30	dynamos, ~~Frigidaires~~ réfrigérateurs		30 bouteilles de Rhum
0h15	cables et tentes	1h30	Fraiseuses, moteurs électriques

A list of everything from radio equipment to shirts, army boots to milling machines. The word "Frigidaires" is crossed out, replaced by "refrigerators" in Mister Casterade's handwriting. I can make out Papa's scrawled signature at the bottom of the page.

★

I went to school on Petits-Hôtels Street, very close to home. Papa would walk me there after he rolled up the shop's steel shutter.

Every morning, we met Mister Casterade walking down Hauteville Street to the office of "CASTERADE & CERTITUDE Exp.–Trans."

"See you in a few minutes, Raymond," my father said.

"See you soon, Georges."

And his long chest would glide faster and faster down the Hauteville Street hill.

We would reach the school, and Papa would pat me on the shoulder.

"Good luck, Catherine. And don't worry if you make spelling mistakes like your Papa. . ."

I now understand that he wasn't saying this from any lack of interest in his daughter's education. He knew that Mister Casterade frightened me with his constant speeches and his lectures about spelling, and he, Papa, was trying to cheer me up.

I ate at the school cafeteria two days a week, and on the other days I had lunch with Papa at the Picardie, a local restaurant on Chabrol Street. Mister Casterade ate lunch there, too. Papa and I would stand on the street corner and watch for him, then wait for about ten minutes after he went into the restaurant so we wouldn't have to sit at the same table. Papa wanted to be alone with me and was afraid that Casterade would start talking about disasters, morality, and spelling. I think Papa arranged it so the restaurant owner gave us the table that was farthest from Casterade's.

At the door of the Picardie, Papa would say:

"Let's take off our glasses, Catherine. That way we'll have an excuse for not seeing Casterade."

Papa often did business with people who would come and sit at our table after we had eaten.

I listened to them talk, but didn't understand everything they said. They were dark-haired men who wore old overcoats. Among them was a red-headed man with gold-rimmed glasses, who would listen to Papa, slack-jawed. I remember his name was Chevreau. One day, Papa told him:

"So, Chevreau, would you be interested in fifty seats from a Constellation?"

Chevreau's eyes widened.

"What kind of seats?"

"Constellation seats. It's an aeroplane, as you know."

"What in the world would I do with them?"

"Well, you could turn them into cinema seats."

Chevreau stared at my father, slack-jawed as usual.

"You know, you really have an imagination. You amaze me, Certitude. Well, all right, I'll take them . . . I'm really amazed."

I could read so much admiration for Papa in Mister Chevreau's eyes that I was amazed, too.

One afternoon, I asked Papa just exactly what he did.

"How can I explain, darling? To help move goods across Europe, each country has what are called shipping firms, and they are headed by . . . Well, to put it more simply, let's say people send me crates and packages. I keep them in the shop. I send them to other people. I get more packages. And so forth . . ."

He took a drag on his cigarette.

"Let's just say I'm in the package business."

When April came, Papa would accompany me to the square in front of Saint Vincent de Paul Church. I would meet a couple of my schoolmates and play there until six o'clock. Papa sat on a bench and generally kept an eye on me while darkhaired men with moustaches and old overcoats — the same ones as in the restaurant, and Chevreau, too — would sit down next to him on the bench, one after another. They talked while Papa took notes in a notebook.

At dusk, we walked down Hauteville Street hand in hand.

"Casterade will be in a bad mood," Papa said. "He can't understand why I make business appointments in the square. It's stupid; the weather's so nice, I get much more work done outdoors."

Casterade would be waiting for Papa in the back of the shop. And indeed, he was usually in a very bad mood.

"Has work been going well, Raymond?" Papa asked.

"Someone has to work around here."

His chest stiffened.

"What about you, young lady?" he asked dryly. "What French poets did you study in school this afternoon?"

"Victor Hugo and Verlaine."

"Same as usual. But they aren't the only ones. Poetry is very vast. For example. . ."

This was no time to cross him.

Papa would sit down at his desk. I remained standing, arms folded.

From an inside pocket, Mister Casterade would pull one of the collections of poems he had written.

"I'm going to give you an example of real French metre."

Then he would read his poems to us in a monotonous voice, beating time with his hand. I still remember the first lines of one poem he was particularly fond of:

Betty with your alabaster neck, and you, Marie Josée,
Do you still remember the promises we made
In Castelnaudary, on those autumn nights. . .

I would sit on Papa's lap and eventually doze off. Much later Papa would wake me up. Night had fallen.

"He's gone," Papa would say, sounding exhausted. "You can put your glasses back on."

Then I helped him roll down the shop's steel shutter.

In the mornings, Papa would wake me up. He would have made breakfast, which was waiting on our little table. He would open the shutters, and I could see him from the back, framed by the window. He looked out over the landscape of roofs, and way in the distance, to the glass dome of the Gare de l'Est train station. As he knotted his tie, he would say, in a thoughtful or sometimes very resolute tone, "Life, it's just you and me."

While Papa shaved, we always played the same game: he would chase me through the whole apartment, trying to smear my face with shaving cream.

Afterwards, we would carefully wipe our glasses, which were spattered with flecks of shaving cream.

One Sunday, we were eating breakfast when we heard the shop's doorbell ring. I helped Papa roll up the steel shutter. A big lorry with a canvas tarp with Spanish writing on it was parked in front of the shop, and three men were starting to unload crates from it onto the pavement. Papa got them to carry the crates inside, then phoned the boarding house where Mister Casterade lived. The three men gave Papa a receipt to sign, and the lorry roared off.

Papa and Mister Casterade opened the crates, which were full of statuettes of ballet dancers. The statuettes in some of the crates were broken, and we put the pieces on the shop's shelves. Then Papa nailed up the remaining crates and went to the telephone, where he talked in a foreign language.

When he hung up the receiver, Mister Casterade said:

"Careful Georges; you're getting in over your head. That receipt you signed won't cut the mustard with French customs. Remember that batch of a thousand Austrian snow boots you sneaked through customs? Those snow boots nearly got you sent up the river. If it hadn't been for me, you would have wound up behind bars."

But my father had taken off his glasses, and said nothing. That evening, a different lorry came to pick up the crates full of dancers. Only the broken statuettes remained. For fun, Papa and I glued the pieces back together and lined the dancers up on the shelves, one by one. Looking at all those rows of dancers, Papa said, "Catherine, darling, would you like to be a dancer, like Mama?"

I remember my first dance lesson. Papa chose a school in the neighbourhood, on Maubeuge Street. The teacher, Madame Galina Dismailova, walked over to me and said, "You'll have to dance without your glasses."

In the beginning, I envied my classmates who didn't wear glasses. Everything was simple for them. But as I thought about it, I realised I had the advantage of living in two different worlds, depending on whether I was wearing my glasses or not. And the world of dance wasn't just real life, but a world where you jumped or did entrechats instead of just walking. It was a dream world, like the soft, blurry one I saw without my glasses.

As we were leaving that first lesson, I said to Papa:

"You know, dancing without my glasses doesn't bother me at all."

Papa seemed surprised by my firm tone.

"If I could see normally without glasses, I wouldn't dance nearly as well. It's an advantage."

"You're right," said Papa. "I was the same way, when I was young. People will see a kind of misty softness in your eyes when you don't wear glasses. It's called charm."

My class met every Thursday, and Papa came with me. The dance studio's big plate-glass windows faced the Gare du Nord train station.

The mothers of the other students sat on a long bench covered with red vinyl. Papa, the only man among those women, sat off by himself at the end of the bench. From time to time, he would look out the window at the Gare du Nord, at the lights on the platforms, at the trains leaving for faraway places. They went all the way to Russia, he said, the country our teacher Madame Dismailova came from.

She had a very strong Russian accent. She would say:

"Catherine Cherrichi-toode . . . Fondoo . . . Tendoo, pas de cheval . . . Attitoude . . . Open second position . . . Feefth position . . . Pied dans la main . . . Étendez . . . Change sides."

One Thursday evening I left my glasses at the dance school. Since Papa had work to do, I went to Maubeuge Street by myself to get them. I knocked on the door, but nobody answered, so I knocked at the caretaker's. She gave me the spare key to the studio. I switched on the light as I went in. The dim glow from a lamp on the piano left parts of the room in shadow. It felt strange to see the big deserted studio and the piano with its empty chair way at the back. My glasses were lying on the bench. A pale light shone through the window, the glow from the Gare du Nord platforms.

So I decided to dance by myself. It only took a little imagination to hear the piano music and Madame Dismailova's voice in the silence:

"Open second position . . . Feefth position . . . Pied dans la main . . . Fondoo . . . Tendoo . . . Pas de cheval . . ."

When I stopped dancing, the silence returned. I put my glasses on. Before leaving the studio, I stood for a moment by the big window, looking at the platforms of the Gare du Nord.

I found a photo from those days, taken by Chevreau, the red-headed man with gold-rimmed glasses who worked with Papa. It was Thursday afternoon, before we left for my dance lesson. You can see me in front of the shop, between Papa and Mister Casterade. Casterade was in a good mood that day, and he's doing a dance step to imitate me.

On the right of the photo, you can just make out a woman; I've only recently started to remember her. One evening, she was in Papa's office and as she was leaving I heard her say:

"I'll see you soon, Georges."

I asked Papa who she was. He seemed embarrassed.

"Oh, nobody. She's an air stewardess . . ."

Twenty years later, when I showed him the photo and pointed to the woman standing next to us, he looked skyward and said the same thing:

"Oh, she was an air stewardess . . ."

My only friend from dance lessons was a little girl who came to Madame Dismailova's every Thursday by herself, without her mother. She spoke to me first.

"You're lucky to wear glasses. I've always wanted to. Can I try them on?"

She put on my glasses and looked at her reflection in the big studio mirror that Madame Dismailova used to correct our positions.

When the lesson was over, she asked me and Papa to walk her to the nearest Metro station, Anvers.

A woman was waiting for her near the entrance to the Metro, reading magazines in front of a newspaper stand on Rochechouart Boulevard. She was wearing a raincoat and flat shoes, and a dour expression.

The woman spoke:

"Late as usual, Odile."

"I'm sorry, Miss Sergent."

Odile had explained that Miss Sergent was her nanny.

One evening, before taking the Metro with her, Odile handed me an envelope. Inside was a card with sky-blue printing.

> *Mr and Mrs Ralph B. Ancorena*
> *invite*
> *Georges and Catherine Certitude*
> *to a spring cocktail party*
> *on Friday, 22 April*
> *at 21 Saussaye Boulevard, Neuilly*
> *at five o'clock*
>
> *R.S.V.P.*

Odile had written Papa's and my name on the invitation herself, and I was surprised that Papa didn't realise at the time that she had done it without her parents' knowledge.

"We have to answer right away and accept the invitation," said Papa. "Friday is tomorrow."

He asked Mister Casterade for advice, who told him:

"I'll dictate a letter."

Papa sat down at his typewriter. Puffing out his chest, Mister Casterade began:

Dear Friends:
It is with great pleasure that . . . my daughter and I . . . accept your
. . . very kind invitation . . . We will therefore . . . see you at Saussaye
Boulevard . . . tomorrow.
Sincerely yours,
Georges Certitude and daughter.

" 'And daughter'?" asked Papa, looking surprised.

" 'And daughter'," said Mister Casterade in a tone that brooked no contradiction. "It's a classic turn of phrase."

Papa telephoned Mister Chevreau and asked him to come to the shop. It was a matter of some urgency, he said.

Chevreau came over right away.

"Could you take this letter to Neuilly right now, to Saussaye Boulevard?" Papa asked.

"Right away?" said Chevreau.

"And tomorrow, I'd like you to fetch me and my daughter in your pickup truck and take us to the same address."

"This is a bit sudden, Certitude."

"Listen, Chevreau," said Papa. "I'll give you the first four rows of those Constellation seats for free. Can't you do me this favour?"

"Well, all right," said Chevreau, impressed.

Papa was both nervous and very eager to go to the cocktail party that Odile's parents were giving.

"Very fine people, the Ancorenas," Papa kept saying, in an odd, worldly tone of voice I had never heard before.

After breakfast, we sat on the bench in Saint Vincent de Paul Square while he made plans for the future.

"You know, Catherine, honey, it doesn't take much for life to become more pleasant . . . Not much at all . . . Just a matter of moving in the right circles . . . I'm really anxious to meet the Ancorenas."

After much indecision, Papa put on his striped brown suit. He had first tried on his blue one, but decided it was too formal for a spring cocktail party. In his hand, he carried the soft felt hat he wore on Sundays. And gloves. Mister Chevreau was waiting for us in his truck in front of the shop.

"To Neuilly, Chevreau. 21 Saussaye Boulevard."

It was as if Papa were giving an order to his chauffeur. So, in his rattletrap truck, Mister Chevreau drove us slowly to Neuilly.

We had barely turned into Saussaye Boulevard when Papa said:

"You can stop here and let us out, Chevreau."

"What do you mean? I'll drop you at number 21."

"I'd rather you let us off here. We can walk the rest of the way."

Mister Chevreau could hardly conceal his surprise. We got out of the truck.

"Wait for us here. Not in front of number 21, you understand? We'll be here for an hour or two."

"Whatever you say, Certitude," said Mister Chevreau.

We walked to number 21, which turned out to be a large house with a manicured lawn. Expensive cars were parked in a gravel courtyard off to the left.

Odile was waiting for us at the front door.

"I was afraid you weren't coming."

She took my arm.

"I'm really happy you're here."

She led us through the wide hallway and into a lift whose walls were covered with red velvet.

"This lift is very handsome," said Papa. "I'll have to install one just like it between my office and my apartment."

Papa was showing off, but I could tell he was ill at ease. He kept adjusting the knot of his tie and fiddling with his hat.

We stepped out onto the terrace. Waiters in white jackets were moving between groups of people, carrying trays of fruit juice and cocktails. The women were wearing sheer dresses and the men looked casually sporty. Some of the guests were standing, glass in hand, and others sat under umbrellas. It was sunny, and a spring breeze was blowing. The air felt much fresher than down below. Odile and I were the only children in the crowd.

As if he were drunk, Papa bowed and shook hands with everyone, saying, over and over:

"Georges Certitude. Pleased to meet you. Georges Certitude. Pleased to meet you."

We found ourselves on the edge of the terrace, in a group of very elegant men and women.

"Listen to me, Catherine," Papa whispered, while fiddling with his hat. "You see that slim blond man leaning on the railing? He's one of the country's top fashion designers. And next to him, the man in the riding jodphurs is a polo player from Santo Domingo; he must have come from a match at Bagatelle. That woman, the distinguished-looking one, was married to Sacha Guitry. And the man who's talking is the head of a big liquor company. You see his name everywhere in the Metro: 'DUBO . . . DUBON . . . DUBONNET.'"

Papa was getting more and more excited, and was talking faster and faster.

"That dark-skinned man is Prince Ali Khan. Or at least looks like him. Isn't that Prince Ali Khan, Odile?"

"Er, yes, sir," said Odile, as if she didn't want to contradict him.

Papa tried to join their conversations. His brown suit clashed with everyone else's light, summery clothes.

"I nearly killed myself in the Talbot yesterday evening," said the designer, pointing out a luxury car down below. "But I'll always have a weakness for Talbots."

"And I'll always have one for Delahayes," said the polo player. "I like them because you can never trust their brakes."

Papa held my hand very tightly. I sensed he was getting his nerve up.

"As for myself," he said, trying to sound casual, "I'm sticking with the Citroën."

And he pointed to a big sedan parked at the street corner below.

Nobody seemed to have heard Papa's remark, except one white-jacketed waiter, who was passing with a tray.

"Sir, it looks to me as if someone is stealing your car," he said to Papa.

And in fact, the Citroën took off and disappeared around the corner.

"Of course not," replied Papa. "My chauffeur is just going to get some cigarettes."

Then, turning to the group of elegant people, he returned to the fray.

"The Citroën's best feature," he said, "is its engine."

But this remark, like his previous one, met with general indifference. Papa drank several cocktails to relax. Odile was still standing next to us.

"I'd like to be introduced to your parents. I haven't met them yet," Papa said. Odile blushed.

"Oh, well, you know, they're very busy," she said.

Looking embarrassed, Odile led us through the groups of guests to the other end of the terrace.

A blonde woman wearing sunglasses and a light blue dress and a man with wavy black hair were surrounded by some people who looked just as stylish as the ones Papa had pointed out earlier.

Odile spoke to the blonde woman in a very small voice.

"Mama, I'd like you to meet Mister Certitude."

"Beg your pardon?" said her mother absent-mindedly.

"Delighted to meet you," said Papa with a little bow.

Behind her sunglasses she could barely see him.

"Papa, this is Mister Certitude," said Odile, trying to get the dark-haired man's attention. "And Catherine Certitude . . . You know, my friend from dance lessons."

"Pleased to meet you," said my father.

"Hello," said Odile's father, casually sticking out his hand.

He and his wife went back to the conversation with their friends.

My father stood stock still. He was at a bit of a loss, but hadn't quite lost his momentum.

"We came . . . in a Citroën," he declared.

It was one of those things you just say, without really thinking, the way you might blink your lights on the highway.

Mister Ancorena raised his eyebrows slightly. Behind her sunglasses, Mrs Ancorena hadn't heard a thing.

Odile wanted to show me her room, and when we came back to the terrace, Papa was deep in conversation with a fat man with a moustache. They were speaking a mysterious language I didn't understand. Then the man walked away while spinning an imaginary dial and holding his palm to his ear — a gesture meaning, "We'll talk on the phone."

"Who was that?" I asked Papa.

"Somebody very important who'll be able to help me," he said.

Papa and I found ourselves outside on the pavement. He looked for the truck at the corner of the boulevard. Mister Chevreau was waving at us through the open window. Papa turned round and glanced furtively towards the house's terrace, from which he could hear bursts of talk and laughter.

"I had to play that one just right," said Papa.

As we were walking towards the truck, Odile ran up behind us. "Why did you leave without saying goodbye to me?" She gave us a shy smile, like an apology. "I hope you weren't too bored at the cocktail party."

"Not at all," said Papa. "I made several very important contacts and I appreciate your inviting us." Then his voice became more serious. "Odile, I think you may have given me a leg up in the world. Things are going to be very different for me, thanks to this cocktail party."

"What about your car?"

"It was just stolen," said Papa, sounding very sure of himself.

He leaned over to Mister Chevreau, who was waiting behind the wheel.

"Thank you for coming, my good man. Be kind enough to drive us to the nearest police station so we can report the theft."

Odile had listened to Papa's every word. Our eyes met and she turned very red.

In the following weeks, I didn't see Odile at dance lessons. I felt very sad, and I asked Madame Dismailova if she knew why my friend had disappeared.

"All I know is that they owe me for a month's worth of lessons."

Papa and I tried to look up her telephone number. We couldn't find a single Ancorena in the phone book, or 21 Saussaye Boulevard, either. The listings went straight from number 19 to number 23. So I decided to write her a letter.

"In any case," said Papa, "I'm counting on Tabélion to give me their phone number. Don't be sad, honey. We'll reach Tabélion sooner or later, and you'll see Odile again."

Tabélion . . . That's another name that echoes in my memory, bringing up a wave of feelings. Tabélion must have made quite an impression on Papa: thirty years later, he still carried the man's business card in his wallet. He showed it to me the other evening. The card was a bit yellowed:

René Tabélion

S. E. F. I. C.

1 Lord Byron Street, (8th) É LY.83.50

He was the only guest who spoke to Papa during the entire cocktail party.

"Do you still remember Tabélion, Catherine?"

Yes, I remember him, a round man with a moustache, wearing an open shirt and a crocodile-skin belt, whom Papa had talked to in that mysterious language.

When we returned from Neuilly in Chevreau's truck, Papa told me:

"I will always be grateful to your friend Odile for inviting us. I spent a long time talking with a man named Tabélion. Remember that name, Catherine: Tabélion. Thanks to him, my business is going to take off."

And from then on, I often saw him dialing Élysées 83-50. But no one answered, and Papa would hang up the phone, disappointed. Or I would hear him say:

"Could I speak to Mister René Tabélion? . . . Georges Certitude . . . Oh, he isn't in? Please ask him to call me back."

Tabélion never called back. And yet Papa believed in him with an unshakable faith.

He often told Mister Chevreau:

"You see, people like Tabélion don't just deal in Constellation seats. They handle whole squadrons. And that makes all the difference."

Mister Casterade would ask ironically:

"Well, what about your Tabélion? No news?"

Papa shrugged.

"You wouldn't be able to understand a man of Tabélion's stature."

One winter evening, as we were walking back from my dance lesson, Papa said:

"You know, Catherine, my father was right. He arrived on the train here at the Gare du Nord, and decided to stay in the neighbourhood. He was the one who opened our shop on Hauteville street. He felt the neighbourhood was right because of the train stations; it would be handy if you felt like leaving . . . What do you say we leave? Wouldn't you like to travel? See new places?"

The last time we went to the dance lesson, Papa told me:

"It's funny, Catherine, but I used to know your teacher, Madame Dismailova. She doesn't recognise me, because I'm not as young as I used to be. And she's changed a lot too. I haven't always worked in business. In the old days, Catherine, I was a fairly handsome young man, and to earn spare cash I used to do walk-ons at the Casino de Paris. One night, they asked me to stand in for one of the lifters. That's what you call the men who carry the dancers in the show. And you know, Catherine, your mother was the dancer I was supposed to carry. This was before we met. I lifted her in my arms the way they showed me, stumbled on stage without my glasses . . . and boom! I tripped and fell. We came crashing down together. Your mother started laughing so hard, she couldn't stop. They had to bring down the curtain. She liked me a lot. It was at the Casino de Paris that I also met your teacher, Madame Dismailova. She danced in the show."

Then Papa, as if he were afraid someone might be following us down Maubeuge Street, slowed down and leaned towards me.

"Well, Catherine," he said in a very low voice, almost a whisper, "she wasn't called Galina Dismailova in those days, but just plain Odette Marchal. She wasn't Russian either; she came from Saint-Mandé, where her parents, who were very nice people, owned a little restaurant. Odette used to invite us there, your mother and me, when the Casino de Paris was closed. She was a good friend. And she didn't have a Russian accent — none at all."

Papa sat down on the red vinyl bench with the other students' mothers and the lesson began.

I listened to Madame Dismailova, whose name was Odette Marchal, say in her Russian accent:

"Fondoo . . . Tendoo . . . Pas de cheval . . . Open second position . . . Feefth position . . ."

I would have liked to hear her real voice.

The dance lesson ended about seven o'clock in the evening, and Madame Dismailova said to us:

"Goodbye, children. See you next Thurrrsday."

In the stairway I whispered to Papa:

"You should have talked to her and called her by her real name."

"You mean I should have said, 'Hello, Odette, how are things in Saint-Mandé?' "

He was silent for a moment, then added:

"No, I could never do that to her. You have to let her dream, her and her customers."

One morning, I went to get the mail as usual to give to Papa, because I was always impatient to see if we would get our two letters from America. Papa's was very thick. In my letter, Mama had written:

Dear Catherine,
I think the three of us will be together again very soon.
Hugs and kisses,
Mama

Sitting at his desk, Papa read his letter from Mama very carefully. Later on the way to school, he said:

"The news from America is excellent."

That same day, Mister Casterade wanted to read us a poem, so we were in the office listening to him. His monotonous voice and his hand beating time were like a lullaby. I could hardly keep my eyes open.

"In Castelnaudary, on those autumn nights . . ."

I had taken off my glasses and was about to fall asleep when Papa suddenly interrupted him:

"Excuse me, Raymond, but it's seven-thirty and I'm taking my daughter to eat at Charlot's, the Shellfish King."

Mister Casterade's chest stiffened. He gave us a disdainful look, and slowly closed his book of poems.

"It's a strange world," he said. "A strange world, where Charlot the Shellfish King is more important than a French poet. Where people prefer a dozen oysters to a well-turned Alexandrine. Well, I hope you enjoy the meal."

Papa cleared his throat. When he spoke, it was in a very solemn voice:

"Raymond, I have something very important to tell you. My daughter and I are leaving for America."

I was so astonished to hear what my father had just announced that I put on my glasses right away to be sure I wasn't dreaming. Mister Casterade stood frozen in front of the office door.

"For America? You're leaving for America?"

"Yes, Raymond."

Mister Casterade collapsed onto his swivel chair.

"What about me?" he asked in a hollow voice. "Have you thought about me?"

"I have thought about you, Raymond. It's very simple. I'm giving you the shop. We'll sleep on it and talk it over tomorrow."

Papa took my arm and we walked out of the shop, leaving Mister Casterade sitting at his desk, mechanically repeating, as if he couldn't quite believe it:

"For America . . . For America . . . Who do they think they are?"

"Catherine, darling, I invited you to the restaurant tonight because I wanted to discuss this trip with you. It's true, we're leaving for America. For America, where we'll be with your Mama."

Papa called Charlot the Shellfish King's waiter over and ordered me a Peach Melba for dessert. Then he lit a cigarette.

"You see, Catherine, when your Mama went back to America, three years ago, I was very sad. But she wanted me to live there, in her own country. I promised her we would join her as quickly as we could, just as soon as I wrapped up my business affairs here in France. Well, the time has come. The three of us will all be together in America. Anyway, your Mama predicted this would happen. As soon as we met, a long time before you were born. When she was still dancing with Miss Maekers' ballet company, she used to tell me: 'Albert,' — I called myself Albert in those days — 'we're going to get married, we're going to have a little girl, and we'll live in America.' Your mother was right . . . But don't let that keep you from eating your Peach Melba, it's going to melt. Do you want me to give you your first English lesson?"

So Papa, pronouncing the words very carefully, said:

"In New York, a Peach Melba is called a 'Peach Melba,' but with an American accent."

It was summer, and it was still light when we left the restaurant. In those days there were platform buses and red-and-black taxis at cab stands in the middle of Place Clichy and at the Gaumont Palace. And chestnut trees.

"Shall we walk home?" said Papa. "It's so nice out, we could go via Montmartre hill."

We walked along Caulaincourt Street, and Papa put his hand on my shoulder.

"I'm going to get us boat tickets for next month, Catherine. In New York, Mama will come and meet us at the dock."

I thought about Mama. The idea of seeing her again after all these years made me very happy.

"Over there, in New York, you'll go to school and learn English. And Mama herself will give you dance lessons. She dances much better than Madame Dismailova, you know. When I met Mama, she was already a star of Miss Maekers' ballet company. And I almost became a 'lifter,' as you know."

We walked down the steps of the Montmartre hill and Papa lifted me up and carried me all the way down Trudaine Avenue, the way he might have done at the Casino de Paris.

"Don't be afraid, Catherine," he told me. "I won't drop you. I've improved since the last time."

During the following week, Papa, Mister Casterade and Mister Chevreau would often meet at the shop. I saw them signing a whole stack of papers. Mister Casterade's voice was becoming more and more demanding.

"Sign here, Chevreau. And you, Georges, here. Don't forget to write, 'As per agreement.'"

One evening, when they were leaving the shop and Papa was still in his office, I heard Mister Casterade tell Mister Chevreau:

"From now on, I want everything to be on the up and up. It's all got to be straightforward. No more little deals under the counter. Strictly legal. Do you understand, Chevreau?"

"That goes without saying."

And Mister Chevreau nodded, looking as if he were sorry about something.

Papa came to fetch me after school, as usual, and we were walking home, along Hauteville Street. To my great surprise, a worker with a ladder had almost finished repainting the shop's sign. It didn't say, "CASTERADE & CERTITUDE Exp.-Trans." any more, but "CASTERADE & CHEVREAU, successor." The red letters of "CASTERADE" gleamed in the sunshine, dwarfing the tiny ones that spelled "CHEVREAU." Mister Casterade was standing very erect in front of the shop's

door with his arms folded. He was wearing the satisfied look
of an owner.

"He could have waited a bit," said Papa. "It's as if we had
already left."

Mister Casterade took us out for a farewell dinner at the Picardie. Chevreau was there. Before we ate, Mister Casterade stood up with a sheet of paper in his hand. It was a poem he had written in honour of our departure.

Standing at the bow, as for America you embark,
Don't forget your friends who in Paris still remain,
New York may be fair and Broadway a starry lane
But few spots can match our own Montsouris Park.

Papa, Mister Chevreau, and I applauded. I was very moved. For the first time in my life, I listened to one of Mister Casterade's poems all the way to the end — and I had kept my glasses on.

After dinner, Papa and I walked towards Saint Vincent de Paul Church. We sat down on one of the benches in the square. "You'll see, Catherine, we'll be happy in America."

He lit a cigarette, leaned his head back, and blew a smoke ring.

"Soon we'll be in the New World. But as Casterade says, we mustn't forget France."

I didn't pay much attention to his remark at the time. But today, after all these years, I seem to hear it clearly, as if I were still that child, on that afternoon, in Saint Vincent de Paul Square.

I often think of my school on Petits-Hôtels Street, of the square where I played with my classmates on those dusty summer afternoons, of our shop with the scale where Papa and I used to weigh ourselves. I think of Mister Casterade, reading us his poems. And of Madame Dismailova, whose real voice I never heard.

We always stay the same, and the people we have been in the past go on living until the end of time. So there will always be the little girl called Catherine Certitude, who is still walking with her father through the streets of the 10th *arrondissement* of Paris.

Yesterday was Sunday, and my daughter and I went to visit my parents in Greenwich Village. They're together for good now, even though Mama often threatens to leave because she gets fed up with "Papa's deals," as she says. Papa's new business partner, Mister Smith, who is as persnickety as Mister Casterade was, agrees with her completely.

The taxi drops us off in front of the tall brick building where they live. High above us, I can see Papa's silhouette in one of their apartment windows. He seems to be tying his tie. Maybe he is thinking of me, saying to himself:

"Life, it's just you and me."